KU-345-332

Amy's Three Best Things

Philippa Pearce &
Robin Bell Corfield

PUFFIN BOOKS

For Sally ~ P.P.

For Ruth ~ R.B.C.

PUFFIN BOOKS

Published by the Penguin Group
Penguin Books Ltd, 80 Strand, London WC2R 0RL, England
Penguin Putnam Inc., 375 Hudson Street, New York, New York 10014, USA
Penguin Books Australia Ltd, 250 Camberwell Road, Camberwell, Victoria 3124, Australia
Penguin Books Canada Ltd, 10 Alcorn Avenue, Toronto, Ontario, Canada M4V 3B2
Penguin Books India (P) Ltd, 11 Community Centre, Panchsheel Park, New Delhi – 110 017, India
Penguin Books (NZ) Ltd, Cnr Rosedale and Airborne Roads, Albany, Auckland, New Zealand
Penguin Books (South Africa) (Pty) Ltd, 24 Sturdee Avenue, Rosebank 2196, South Africa

Penguin Books Ltd, Registered Offices: 80 Strand, London WC2R 0RL, England

www.penguin.com

First published 2003
1 3 5 7 9 10 8 6 4 2

Set in Cantoria 16/24 pt and Goudy Old Style 18pt

Manufactured in China

British Library Cataloguing in Publication Data
A CIP catalogue record for this book is available from the British Library

ISBN 0-670-91095-3

One day Amy said, “I’d like to go and see Granny soon. I’d like to go all by myself, and I’d like to stay the night.”

Her mother said, “Are you sure, Amy?” for Amy had not been away from home by herself before.

“Of course I’m sure,” Amy said crossly. “In fact, I’ll stay two nights. No. I’ll stay three.”

Amy packed a bag with her teddy bear and her pyjamas and all the other ordinary things she needed.

Then she put in three more things.

Those are my three best things for a visit, she thought.

"What will you do while I'm away?" Amy asked her mother.

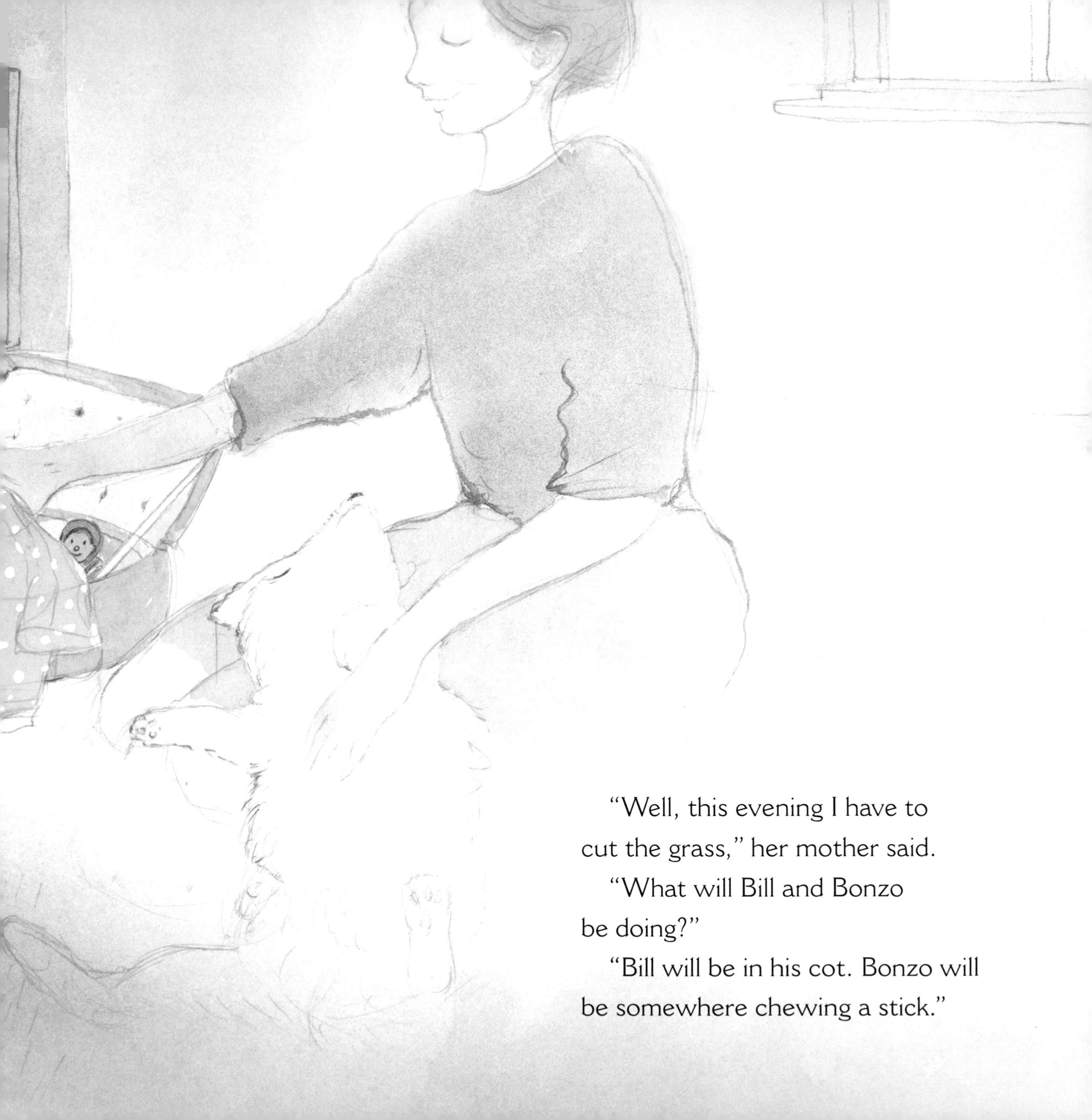

"Well, this evening I have to cut the grass," her mother said.

"What will Bill and Bonzo be doing?"

"Bill will be in his cot. Bonzo will be somewhere chewing a stick."

When she reached Granny's house, Amy unpacked her bag. But she didn't take out her three best things because they were secret. Then it was time for bed. Amy soon fell asleep, but later she woke. It was still daylight. She missed her mother and Bill and Bonzo. She wanted her own home.

Then she remembered
her three best things.

She got out of bed and fetched the first: a little stripey mat from beside her bed at home. Amy laid the mat on the floor by her bed in Granny's house. She sat on the edge of the bed with her feet on the mat.

At first, Amy didn't feel any better. Then she noticed a tingling in her feet. She stood up on the mat. It seemed to shift beneath her. She sat down on the mat, only just in time, for it was beginning to move. The mat was rising, slowly at first. Then, in a rush, it rose much higher.

It flew towards the window, and the window opened wide,

and Amy, on the magic mat, sailed out into the summer air.

The mat flew smoothly and fast in the direction of home.
And here was her house and there was the garden and her mother had just finished cutting the lawn.

She was scolding Bonzo, who had chewed up a stick all over the new-cut grass.

Then Amy wanted to see what Bill was doing,
and the mat took her to his bedroom window.

There he was, asleep in his cot with his knitted rabbit up to his cheek.

Amy wasn't feeling unhappy any more. Swiftly, the mat turned and carried her back – back to her granny's house, in through the window

and down to the floor by Amy's bed. It was just an ordinary little stripey mat again.

The next day Amy and her granny went on an expedition and came back late and tired. Amy fell asleep quickly, but moonlight on her face woke her. She sat up, missing home all over again. She missed her mother and Bill and Bonzo.

Then she remembered her three best things. She got out of bed and fetched the second: a tiny wooden horse from her bookshelf at home.

Amy put the tiny horse on the floor, and it began to grow. As it grew, it pawed the ground and snorted with impatience.

When the horse was the right size, Amy climbed on to its back and it set off at a gallop – through the air, out of the window and into the moonshiny night.

It whinnied for joy as it rushed towards Amy's house.

As late as this, everyone would be indoors. Amy looked into the sitting room.
There sat her mother, watching television, with Bonzo snoozing at her feet.

In his bedroom, Bill was also asleep
with his knitted rabbit at his cheek.

And now the horse tossed its mane and set off back to Granny's house.

It galloped all the way, and in through Amy's window
and down to her bedside. It became just a tiny wooden horse again.

Amy picked it up
and put it safely on
the mantlepiece.

The next day Amy and her granny stayed mostly indoors, because it rained. This was the last day of Amy's visit. Granny told her that tomorrow her mother would come with Bill and Bonzo to take her home.

"But before you leave," Granny said, "if it stops raining, we could all go to the fair."
"I'd like that," said Amy. "I'd like that very much."

That night Amy
fell asleep to the
sound of rain.
Later, thunder
and lightning
woke her.

She sat up in bed
thinking what a long way
off tomorrow seemed.
She wanted her mother
and Bill and Bonzo NOW.

Then she remembered her three best things. She got out of bed and fetched the third: a little wooden boat from the bathroom at home. As she looked, the boat began to grow, and then to rock as though it were riding on water. When it was big enough, Amy stepped in.

The boat rose and sailed out
through the window, into the stormy night.

Amy was not afraid of the storm,
and the rain did not even dampen her pyjamas.

Through whistling wind and rushing rain, the boat took Amy to her home.

She looked in through the sitting room window,

but the television was switched off. There was no one there,
not even Bonzo. No one was in Bill's room either – his cot was empty.

Last of all, Amy looked in the garage and – sure enough, as she had feared – the car was gone. Then she knew that all her family had gone away without her.

She flung herself down in the bottom of the boat, and cried.

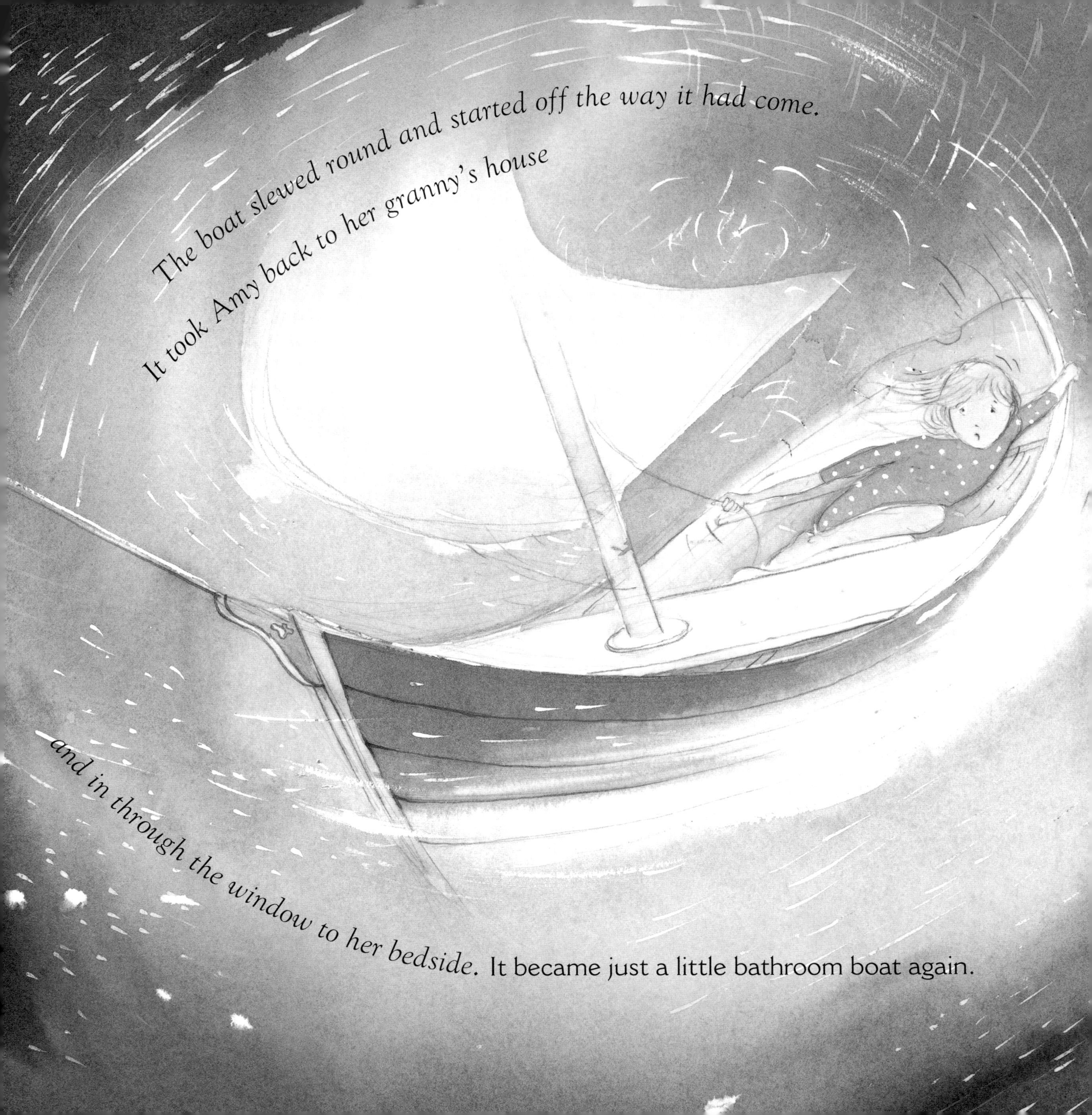

The boat slewed round and started off the way it had come.
It took Amy back to her granny's house

and in through the window to her bedside. It became just a little bathroom boat again.

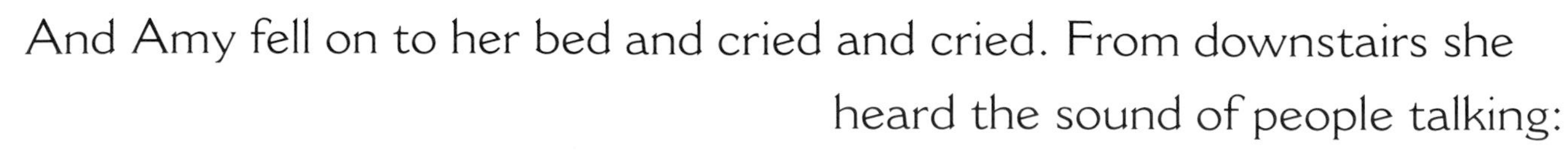

And Amy fell on to her bed and cried and cried. From downstairs she heard the sound of people talking: Granny had visitors. But Amy did not care if they heard her.

From downstairs someone said, "Hush! Listen."

Then Amy heard her mother's voice say, "It's Amy crying!"

Next there were footsteps hurrying upstairs, the bedroom door was flung open and her mother was kneeling beside her, asking, "Amy, whatever is the matter?"

“I missed you all,” said Amy, still crying because she couldn’t stop all at once.

“Well, here we all are,” said her mother. “We came tonight instead of tomorrow morning. We were missing you too.”

She tucked Amy up and kissed her goodnight. “Tomorrow, if it’s fine, we’ll go to the fair.”

And the next day the sun shone, so they all went to the fair. Amy's favourite thing at the fair was the old-fashioned merry-go-round. When the music played, all the animals moved up and down and round in their big circle.

Amy chose to ride a horse. When the music started, she clung on tight and waved goodbye to her family. Then the merry-go-round swirled her off, so that she could no longer see them.

But she knew that they
would still be there when
she came round again.
Of course they would.

And so they were.